It had snowed all night on the Island of Sodor. At Tidmouth Sheds, the engines looked out.

The trees were **white** … the cottages were **white** … and the railway tracks were hidden under a blanket of **white** snow too!

The Fat Controller asked Thomas to deliver firewood to the stations and told Gordon to take some trucks to the Docks.

"You are a strong engine, Gordon," said The Fat Controller, as he left, "but snow is **slippery**. Avoid the hills and puff the long way round."

Gordon pumped his pistons proudly. "I'm going straight to the Docks," he said to Thomas. "I am **strong**. I am the **best**. I can easily steam over any hill I come to."

But Thomas was worried. He'd heard what The Fat Controller had said and he knew that snow could be **dangerous**.

But off Gordon huffed. Soon he came to a hill.

"This hill isn't too steep for me," he boomed. "I'll steam over it."

Gordon chuffed to the top without any problems but going down the other side wasn't so easy. Gordon's wheels **slipped** and **slid** …

… Gordon went **faster** and **faster.**

Spencer was huffing up the hill towards him.

"Slow down, Gordon," Spencer shouted. But Gordon couldn't slow down.

Gordon wheeshed past Spencer, spraying him with slushy snow. **Splish! Splash!**

And on Gordon raced.

Gordon managed to slow down,
but it wasn't long before he came to the
biggest hill on the Island.

"Snow is soft and I am **strong**. It won't
bother me," he muttered.

But as Gordon pushed up the hill through
the snow, it became a snowball.

The snowball grew **bigger** and **bigger** …

Thomas came up behind Gordon on the hill.

"Thank you for clearing the tracks," said Thomas.

But then there was trouble. The giant snowball was **too big** and **too heavy**. Gordon could go no further. Then the snowball began to push Gordon back down the hill again!

"Watch out, Thomas!" he shouted.

Gordon was pushed back **faster** and **faster** …

So Thomas chuffed back **faster** and **faster** …

Until Gordon rolled into a siding and – **crash!** – the snowball **bashed** into Thomas. It knocked him right off the rails!

Gordon tried to shunt Thomas and his trucks of firewood back onto the track. But he wasn't strong enough.

"I'm sorry, Thomas," puffed Gordon, sadly. "I'm not strong, and I'm not the best. I'll find Rocky. He's better at this than me."

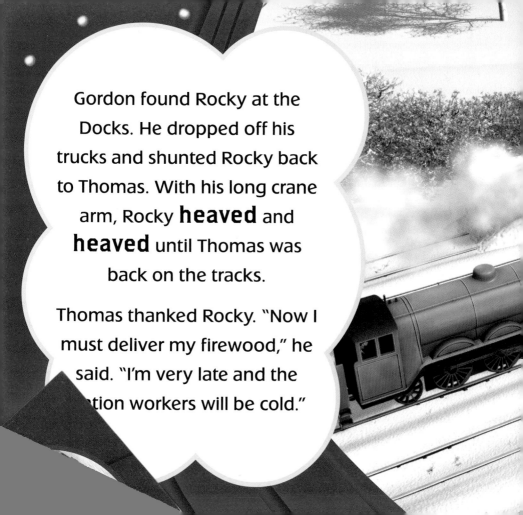

Gordon found Rocky at the Docks. He dropped off his trucks and shunted Rocky back to Thomas. With his long crane arm, Rocky **heaved** and **heaved** until Thomas was back on the tracks.

Thomas thanked Rocky. "Now I must deliver my firewood," he said. "I'm very late and the tion workers will be cold."

"I'll help you, Thomas," said Gordon, kindly. So off they puffed, carefully, through the snow.

Together they delivered firewood to all the stations and when they came to a hill … they always puffed **round** it!

PEEP! PEEP!

The End